EARTHLY QUIETUS

MIKE PEARCE

DEDICATION

This book is dedicated to Vera whose enthusiasm for protecting the environment and the community was the main flame in her life.

CONTENTS

ACKNOWLEDGEMENTS

The author would like to thank Christine Pearce for reading and checking through the manuscript.

PREVIEW

Natalie lived with her Nan who was a pillar of strength for her community in environmental issues. They witnessed changes in environmental issues which became more and more labeled as the fault of human existence. This earth is no stranger to change. It has seen Ice Ages, mass extinctions, as well as tremendous evolutionary adaptations over millions of years.

Everyone expected global warming but ignored the fact that unpredictable weather and disasters were due to the energy from the sun decreasing. The earth was now actually heading towards global cooling and the next Ice Age. The new forms of clean energy would prove a catastrophe.

Winter hung in there, like an invalid
refusing to die. Day after day the ice
stayed hard; the world remained
unfriendly and cold.

Neil Giaman from Odd and the Frost Giants

1 VERA

My name is Natalie and my Nan's name is Vera. I live with my Nana as my parents were both drowned in an accident at sea when I was a baby. My Nan loves me very much and always talks about my parents who said that one day I would be something special. I hold onto this and it helps me to survive this world when things go wrong.

My Nan is special and never seems to stop working. She wants to make the world a better place and fights to make sure it happens. She has a knack of getting funding from organisations for small projects which help our community and sits on committees at the council office to keep an eye on proposed changes. She represented the Local Agenda 21 when it was first started and brought together groups from all quarters who felt that something better could be done for this world. Now today it seems that this agenda is commonplace and many people are fighting for change.

My Nan would read me stories at night. She often would tell me how the earth originated. She said the earth was formed around four and a half billion years ago but there was no oxygen around then but there was nitrogen and carbon dioxide. Its surface was pounded by meteors and strong ultraviolet light killed anything in sight. She made me laugh when she said I was made of carbon like the first simple organisms but these would rely on chemicals to survive and probably lived and gained energy from under sea vents. She took great pleasure in telling me how she once visited the Danokil depression in Ethiopia where bacteria could survive in water temperatures of over 80 degrees centigrade.

I loved to listen to her. When she spoke she was so serious as if she needed me to know this information but I must admit I often fell asleep as she carried on. The earth she said is always changing

She would take a deep breath and I knew what she was going to say, she would repeat the same thing forgetting she had already said it. "The earth has always changed and will change again," she took another deep breath. "The oxygen that we depend on triggered life's explosion. It first came from single celled plankton in the sea which exploded in numbers with the iron present. The presence of trees taking in carbon dioxide also increased the oxygen in the air." She took another breath, and said, "animals became huge."

My eyes were closing and I fell asleep. Sometimes I had nightmares. Most parents would tell you stories of princes and wonderful mythical creatures such as unicorns, but my Nan would tell me about giant six foot centipedes, scorpions and dragonflies and how dinosaurs grew large as they breathed better than the other lizard like forms that were around.

2 EXTINCTION

My Nan and I were members of a wildlife society which aimed to protect species on our earth. We often took part in marches and protests. But most people did seem not interested as it did not affect them personally and the animals were far off in other countries. Vera's husband would keep reminding us much to his wife's annoyance, that extinction of species is not a recent phenomenon. There has always been background extinction. It was an integral part of every species since life first appeared. He said we've already had five mass extinctions and each time at least three quarters of plant species were lost. Even though sometimes, given the right conditions, evolution was fast, more than 99% of species that ever existed are no longer around today. "Look," he said, "over one million living species have been described to date, insects being a third of them, but it is believed there are seven times that number still waiting to be discovered."

I asked, "Will we become extinct?" He said. "It depends on the severity of changes and how these last. But we are always, as with other life, affected by sudden disasters and these can kill even the best adapted species in an instant. Life is affected by the roll of the dice and chance plays a great part.

"Think of when we sheltered in caves. We still survived   even when plants were few. Animals provided us with food." He rubbed his hands together. We domesticated some so we did not need to hunt or risk out lives anymore. Clever us eh?

My Nan shut him up. She was a strict vegetarian and any mention of eating animals made her feel queasy. Want some cake? she said and scuttled off to the kitchen to fetch some.

3 THE YEAR 2000

It was now approaching the year 2000. There was an apprehension about moving into the new millennium. In the past the Rev Thomas Malthus had said that population growth will deplete all food. This led to Darwin's theory of struggle for existence. The book Limits to Growth had also made us worry about whether we could survive and people were giving warnings. Nostradamus had also predicted the end of the world and I remember sitting with my Nan in our front room by the fire watching the television as celebrations of the new year were about to begin. It was thick snow outside and quiet very quiet I half expected the whole world to collapse on the last stroke of midnight as predicted.

These worries have always been in people's minds but nothing happened. Especially where in 1970 computer models predicted that the burning of fossil fuels would trigger another Ice Age. There was an ice scare and people were told they were quickly entering the next Ice Age based on cooling effects from long term measurements. My Nan Vera said that there is always a way of redressing the balance, nature knows best and one cannot fathom the ingenuity of man to survive. "Think how." She said, "some humans survived in the Ice Ages, many went to coastal caves where food and higher temperatures existed. People move just as the Egyptians moved when tributaries of the Nile dried up. We are survivors, civilisations may fall but their descendants are still with us."

4 THE YEAR 2021

I was now married to a meteorologist. I had two small children and worked part time in the council in admin. My husband to some would seem not attractive. My Nan always said that even humans choose mates on their attractiveness (Love is Blind, Darwin's beauty rather than brawn) and I had not chosen a partner to help the survival of our race or because of his abilities Times had changed really changed, there was anger growing in the population that we all should do something. Gone was the gentle approach of saving the environment by not dropping litter and putting a brick in the toilet to save water. Green fairs were more environmental protests. We are now in an interglacial period but many believe because of our activities, it increased carbon dioxide levels, land exploitation or pollution that we are heading towards the sixth extinction

People now really believed that doomsday was upon us and cries in demonstrations and the press rang out with-

Climate change is a serial killer

A quarter of the world's species will be lost in 50 years

The world is like a discarded toy that can't be mended

It's like Chernobyl, apocalyptic decline

This is the age of destruction

A vortex into chaos

The world is overrun by humans

Collapsing world

Devastating future

A fading natural world

Conservation emergency

Might as well go to another planet

It's offensive to God

Moment of crisis

Last chance now

We are facing the moment of truth

A crime is being committed

Taking our eye off the prize

Chiselling away at our safety net

Our lives depend on this fight

It is the end of days the antichrist is here

We are committed to extinction

World doomsday is coming

We are in an intermediate stage to a human grave yard

We are on the escalator to extinction

We were warned not to eat meat and that cows and termites were increasing harmful global gases

The last coal mine in England was now closed. We became more reliant on coal and even oil from other countries.

The doomsday clock, as set up in 1947 in case of nuclear attack, still lies waiting to move, its hand towards midnight, but now other triggers are contributing towards this global calamity. Over one thousand disasters in the last fifty years have been attributed to being caused by a change in climate. Many are patiently watching, waiting to stamp the terms climate change/ global warming on any adverse event occurring however small.

Both my Nan and I have always wanted to help animals. We adopted a tiger, a rhino and even a penguin and received a cuddly toy and information on how these animals were doing. But we knew that one day some of these would be extinct because of humans or changes in the environment.

We both knew humans could not protect all the species from extinction. Where life exists it will always be present. Most recent extinctions happened during the 1930s and the number of extinctions have been declining since then. We just had to go to the Natural History Museum London to see the evidence of this.

The earth once had been a huge snowball and now ice was restricted to the poles and mountains but would this last?

Life had been transported to other regions by land bridges and moving tectonic plates. Animals in these new environments thrived or died and even multiplied where there were no predators Changes in environment can also mean a difference in climate. This may shift seasons and mean animals and plants may develop earlier and can also have more offspring. My Nan and I have noticed how trees and shrubs are growing bigger over the years and leaf cover and berries and seed production is increasing. The squirrels now have abundant acorns. "Look at the differences," he said, "in different climates. Mountain species may have bigger lungs. Animals in the poles have stores of fat and can be larger to retain heat."

I knew animals could adapt. I remember when we had milk bottles and the blue tits would peel off the silver foil tops to drink the milk. I'd seen gulls living inland on houses and feeding on landfill sites, and the increase in sea life living on manmade structures under the sea. Life can adapt. Cities are not always barriers to animals. They can creep in at night or live in new habitats. It is important to comprehend that the same species may exist in several locations so one can recolonize or be reintroduced even becoming pests. Where there is connectivity, humans and animals can move to warmer or cooler areas which can encourage greater diversity and other benefits

There is a positive and negative pattern to environmental change.

Animals and humans together have also always taken the risk of living in dangerous places where past disasters or current oppression is occurring. Often land is cheaper, more available and very fertile, as seen in areas of known volcanic activity. On the other hand they may be forced to live in such areas through civil disturbance, religious or racial prejudice and war. The spread of a new idea can often kindle a flame which burns quickly and flares up into an unstoppable belief just like Christianity. Science is taken by some as a god, here to save us but not forgive us. My Nan and I were aware of the changes to come but felt like others that we should comply but little did we know the consequences.

5 THE YEAR 2030

My Nan is now not so mobile. She bravely carried out her civic duties even though her eye sight was failing. She was special, oh so special and the fire that grew in her belly was still there but now only a flicker. I took her out to the beach in the summer. It was crowded with children playing in the sand. Warning notices were everywhere. People were being made to leave the beach if they dropped any litter. Water quality notices were in great detail so many were wary of going into the sea to swim. There were no gulls flying past. Those by the sea had long been considered vermin, pest and poisoned. The sparrows that gathered in the garden bushes no longer sang, being driven away by magpies.

We moved up to the railings. The sky was a beautiful blue with cotton wool clouds floating past. We could feel the sun on our cheeks but not so hot as usual.

"Dear," said my Nan, "what is that out at sea. It spreads right along on either side."

" Wind turbines," I said. "The whole vista was now turbines, blotting the landscape like some industrial plant."

We now had rules and laws which were made to compensate for our selfish attitudes on how we lived. We were under extreme pressure to keep them.

Many of our well known animals were now extinct. The large mammals were the first to go unlike those creatures which had better chances of survival and chance of adaptation as their lifespans are short with many generations. They had tried cloning but lifespans were reduced and other complications shortened their lifespan. They even had tried changing the genes with animals from the past but this hybrid often did not survive in the new environment. Maintaining old breeds was often not economic so projects were dropped. My Nan said, "Creating monsters from the past may be all well and good for a P.T Barnum spectacular circus like show but contributes little to the resurrection of a viable ancient species."

.

It was often said in the past "It does not matter, let's save money, things have changed". But they haven't. Things had got worse through neglect. This kind of oblivion resulted in disasters, for example removal of trees leading to unstable ground and landslides, building houses on flood plains, and ceasing the cleaning out of drainage channels resulting in flooding. These disasters are often then blamed on changes in climate. The Aberfan disaster where coal spoil waste placed on top of a mountain slope slid down onto a school killing hundreds of children was blamed on excessive rainfall. If this happened today some would direct the blame to climate change and global warming even though there were no regulations at the time on the accepted height of the coal waste spoil.

High profile people, people in the public eye from all disciplines, be it music, sport, television etc. or organisations, had been recruited for persuasion. People become servants to these and listened to those who blame others or things

The law of the jungle exists in humans as well as in animals. Some people like to be led, told to stand up to their rights. Leaders play out their visions making sure they control others to carry out these visions. Guilt and shame are used to sell their thoughts. Headline grabbers producing assertions not based on scientific honesty were now common and not backed by evidence. Now the small spark from the 1970s had grown into a fire but what would happen when it was put out?

6. THE YEAR 2035

My Nan had passed away. We had driven to the crematorium in an electric hearse. Slowly and silently it made its way through the snow covered empty streets. It was summer but felt more like winter and we did not stay long at the graveside.

People everywhere were in winter clothes. We hadn't seen the full sun for months. Everyone was questioning why the climate was not getting hotter as predicted.

We knew we were in an inter-glacial period. The earth had experienced many Ice Ages and humans just survived the last one. We are now at the start of the next one People need to think outside the box. Environmental changes are just blips on the earth's radar

. It was said that perhaps climate is not the result of humans but is determined by solar activity, and changes in the earth's orbit and gravitational fields. Our satellite monitoring the sun's activity showed that solar energy was decreasing and we had now entered a grand solar minimum greater than seen in the past. The sun's solar flares were less but solar winds are cooling the outer earth's atmosphere. We were told to expect more seismic activity and more unpredictable weather, droughts and more floods. The papers referred to the great frost of January 1709 where temperatures fell to minus 15 degrees centigrade. Rivers and seas froze and even trees exploded. In France there were over six hundred thousand deaths from starvation. All because the energy of the sun diminished and many volcanic eruptions were triggered around the world. Already we were getting records of minus temperatures in the Sahara and Saudi Arabia with massive falls in Russia. Christmas came and, went, we had had no summer.

7 THE YEAR 2036

It was spring but still the sun did not show and ice and snow lay on the ground. The global warming supporters were now quiet but still said things would change. We reached November and suddenly there was a massive fall in temperature. People were freezing; the sea had frozen over wind turbines were not turning. The fields of solar panels were now snow and ice covered but even if not there wasn't any sun to illuminate them. We had no coal or oil to burn as this had been banned a century ago. People struggled to cut down trees in their gardens and parks to burn. Roads were ice covered; electric cars were unable to gain the force to get along them. I screamed out that we should have researched the consequences of global cooling not global warming and build up reserves for the future and devise new technology that will keep us warm.

I sat in my front room and peered out of my ice coloured window. Bang, something hit the glass hard. I went out of the front door. It was a small bird, its wings frozen together. I could see the seagulls use to cold weather struggling to fly as ice crystals clung to their wings. Little did they know they would soon be grounded for good, frozen like garden ornaments on the beach. People were dying from the cold left in their cold houses which had become home freezers. Doors froze over so people were trapped inside their homes. My family huddled together all larger in size because of the many jumpers we had on.

Perhaps we should have invested in nuclear fuel and other forms of energy as well as thinking of living underground like foxes. I wished we lived in a volcanic area but we didn't. There at least there would be some heat gained from geysers and thermal springs. If humans survived that is where they would be, I thought. Also, how many of today's plants and animals would survive this global cooling?

I looked out of the window and saw dotted along the pavement frozen pure white ghastly figures of people who had ventured outside. There was even a woman pushing a pram, her marble like baby frozen in time with no future like the other children in this world.

My husband and children had fallen asleep next to me never to wake again. I opened my mouth and tried to cry for the world but couldn't. Slowly my sight faded

as my eyes turned bright white with the cold.

To see other publications below by the author visit **snappysnappybooks.com or just search Dr Mike Pearce Amazon books.**

Many of these books in these volumes are also published individually

SNAPPY SNAPPY COLLECTIONS:

Volume 1. BUSINESS AND SELF CONFIDENCE

How to be a Successful Business Weed
Clingers, Creepers and Scramblers
How to Deal with Life's Snakes and Ladders
Trust-Nothing but a Must
Know Your Students and Build Your Image
Hidden from the Heart but not Forgotten
More Pens for Pops
Charity Shops

Volume 2. IDENTITIES, HANG UPS AND CONCERNS

I Herring Gull
Pulvi Royal
I am Termite
Go Fat Go
Make up-Revealed
Fertility Stones and Chocolate Eggs
Captain Grottbuster versus the Grey World

The kittiwakes Warning
Wastefulness-Bone and Urine
Tails, Tales
A slice of Slang with a touch of Cockney and a drop
of Dorset
Mr Hamstrings Dinner

Volume 3. HORROR AND HISTORY

The Living Fossils
My Therizinosaurus
Human Termites eat London
Pigeons Splat London
Glass Anemones Tentacle-ize London
Beware of Cucumbers, Apples and Pigs
The Cornish Urchin
Baby Toes
Googolplex of Mice
Screaming Alley
The Night Mare
Queen Rat on Deadman's Island
Dead Donkey Lane
Old Mother Nature laughed and Laughed
The Plaster Room

Volume 4. RELIGION AND HOPEFULNESS

Pattern for Purpose God's and Man's designs
The Littlest Oyster
Tuppeny Hangover
In a Dark, Dark Corner was the Holy Ghost
The Little Shepherd Boy's Gift

Spider in the Tomb
The Sparrows' Last Soul
The Pawnbroker's Souls
The Red Church Doll
The Boy who found Christmas
The Eggstraordinary Easter Egg
Little Mary
Shepherd's Purse
Sitting next to Angels
The White Lily-St Mildred-Patron Saint of Thanet

Volume 5. TIDE AND TIME

The Shell Man
The Shell Lady
The Watcher on the Fal
The Rock Pool
A Call under the Sea
Pocket full of Starfish
The Scrofula Infirmary
Till my Lips were Salt as Brine
The Man with a Book on his Head
Coloured Bricks
The Girl Under the Paeony Tree
Nothing but Leaves
The China Blackbird
The Man who Collected Figures
The Rusty Gate
Time Runs Dry (a play set in a care home)

Volume 6. FAIRY TALES AND POEMS

The Nursery Rhyme Cat
 Cats at Christmas

The Tuppeny Bear
The Giant and the Giraffe Boy
The Giant's Toothpick
The White Cockerel
The Old Pot and the Golden Shoes
Ball Rooms
Exodus to a Leaf
The Forlorn Fruit Fly
Two Sleepy Boys
Mrs Light and Mr Dark
 I'm Just Going to the Bathroom
The Tulip Tree
The Man who always Sprinted
Bits and Bobs (Poems and short stories for children)

Volume 7. A VARIETY OF WOMEN

Photosynthetic Women
Absorbed by a Woman
The Slothful Wife
Betty's Barcodes
Valentines Cards
The Lady loves Red
The Woman who Smelled Books
Boy, Could She Smell!
The Lady who loved Hairspray

Volume 8. **CHRISTMAS BOOKS**

Impy Christmas
The Little Shepherd Boys Gift
The Boy who found Christmas
Oh, father Christmas what yer going to do?
Nothing but leaves
The Tuppeny hangover
The China Blackbird
The Tuppeny Bear
Cats at Christmas
I Hate Christmas

Volume 9. **HIDDEN PERCEPTIONS**

Silhouette on the pier
I'm not a dinosaur
Mr Mucus
The golden steps
Napoleonic Frankenstein

Volume 10. **MANY CURIOUS STORIES**

The house that cries
The paint brush
The man who collected smiles
Jack and the ivy
The stolen baby
The angels quest
The silly isles
Wilderness Way
I am shadow
The lift

Volume11. CHRISTMAS BOOKS 2

Christmas butterfly
The man in the library
City of laughter, city of tears
Blower Armageddon
Happy Christmas
Antman
A fairy journey
The top of the hill
The Christmas visitor
Ring up an angel
The Christmas raindrop

Volume 12.FAITH AND FAME

Fight for Faith (Gordon of Khartoum)
Angel 1818 (James Blundell)
The Saint who carried his head (St. Denis)

Volume 13. A CORNUCOPIA OF SHORT STORIES

The cursing stone
Punch and Judy (New version)
Touch of Kent dialect
One in 20 million
Be a used seed (Finding new horions)
'Open Arse' (The maligned Medlar)
Wings of colour
Elephant pin-cushion

Volume 14 PLANTASTIC

One in twenty million
Be a seed(Finding new horizons)

The open arse (A maligned medlar)
Nothing but leaves
Exodus to a leaf
The tulip tree
Photosynthetic women
Shepherd's purse
 The girl under the paeony tree
Jack and the ivy
Baby toes
Half a flower
How to be a successful business weed
Clingers creepers and scramblers

Volume 15 INSECTASiA
I am termite
Mother of hundreds
The living fossils
Human termites eat London
Brief encounters with insects
Spider in the tomb
The forlorn fruit fly
The Christmas butterfly
Towers of wax
Antman

Volume 16 TA TA TALES
Condiment kiss
Half a flower
Towers of wax
Gee haw whammydiddle
Peeping Tom
Flowers in the snow
One hundred
Life's escalators

Swallowed by a whale
Volume 17 Golden O0jamaflips
Mother loses leaves
Mothers of fertility
A gender fluid tree-The Mulberry
The golden chamber
The golden tongue
The little white stool
The wedding dress
I am white aphid
A letter to Lady Ellhorn
I'm coming for you now
Biscuit man
Left behind

OTHER STAND ALONE PUBLICATIONS at snappysnappybooks.com

Red Fred Cell and Friends (Human Biology - advanced level
Ronnie's Sermon Snippets
Viking Bay-Natural History (Broadstairs, Kent)
The World of Wax
God rest you Merry Scrooge
Napoleonic Frankenstein
Satan's stars
HOP to Heaven
The White Lily-St Mildred-Patron Saint of Thanet
Brexit Rhymes

ABOUT THE AUTHOR

Dr Mike Pearce is a scientist interested in behaviour. He also was a lecturer in human biology and health at a college in Canterbury, Kent. He has written over 100 short stories as well as a many non-fiction and self-help publications

For more information see snappysnappybooks.com